Sing~Along Song

For Jimmy, who's just gotta sing along—J.E.M. ❀ To Sweet Baby James Carswell—L.P.

Viking

Published by Penguin Group

Penguin Young Readers Group, 345 Hudson Street, New York, New York 10014, U.S.A.

Penguin Books Ltd, 80 Strand, London WC2R 0RL, England

Penguin Books Australia Ltd, 250 Camberwell Road, Camberwell, Victoria 3124, Australia

Penguin Books Canada Ltd, 10 Alcorn Avenue, Toronto, Ontario, Canada M4V 3B2

Penguin Books (N.Z.) Ltd, 182-190 Wairau Road, Auckland 10, New Zealand

First published in 2004 by Viking, a division of Penguin Young Readers Group

10 9 8 7 6 5 4 3 2 1

Text copyright © JoAnn Early Macken, 2004
Illustrations copyright © LeUyen Pham, 2004

LIBRARY OF CONGRESS CATALOGING-IN-PUBLICATION DATA IS AVAILABLE
ISBN: 0-670-05890-4

Set in Fink Roman
Manufactured in China
Book design by Nancy Brennan

Sing-Along Song

Written by
JoAnn Early Macken

Illustrated by
LeUyen Pham

Viking

Robin greets the morning from the sycamore tree,
Chirpin' to the risin' sun, her babies, and me.

When I hear that robin sing her cheery-up song,
I burst out singin'! I just gotta sing along.

Cheery day! Mornin', sun!
C'mon, wake up, everyone!

Bee is buzzin' loop-de-loops all around my head,
Searchin' for some nectar in the strawberry bed.

When I hear that bee sing his honey-buzzin' song,
I burst out singin'! I just gotta sing along.

Busy buzz, dizzy fuzz!
Bumble like a bee does!

Squirrel skips and scampers on the front porch rail,
Scoldin' all the neighborhood and flickin' his tail.
When I hear that squirrel sing his chitter-chat song,
I burst out singin'! I just gotta sing along.

Chitter-chat!
Skitter-skat!
Squirrel chatter!
How 'bout that?

Dog lies drowsin' in the middle of the kitchen,
Ears all flappin' and his toes all twitchin'.
When I hear that dog sing his whuffle-woof song,
I burst out singin'! I just gotta sing along.

Whuffle-snuff, woofle-whiff!
Giggle, sniggle, snort, sniff!

Cat stretches out across
  the creaky rockin' chair,
Swattin' at a skeeter
  swoopin' round the air.

When I hear that cat sing
  his yowl-meowlin' song,
I burst out singin'!
  I just gotta sing along.

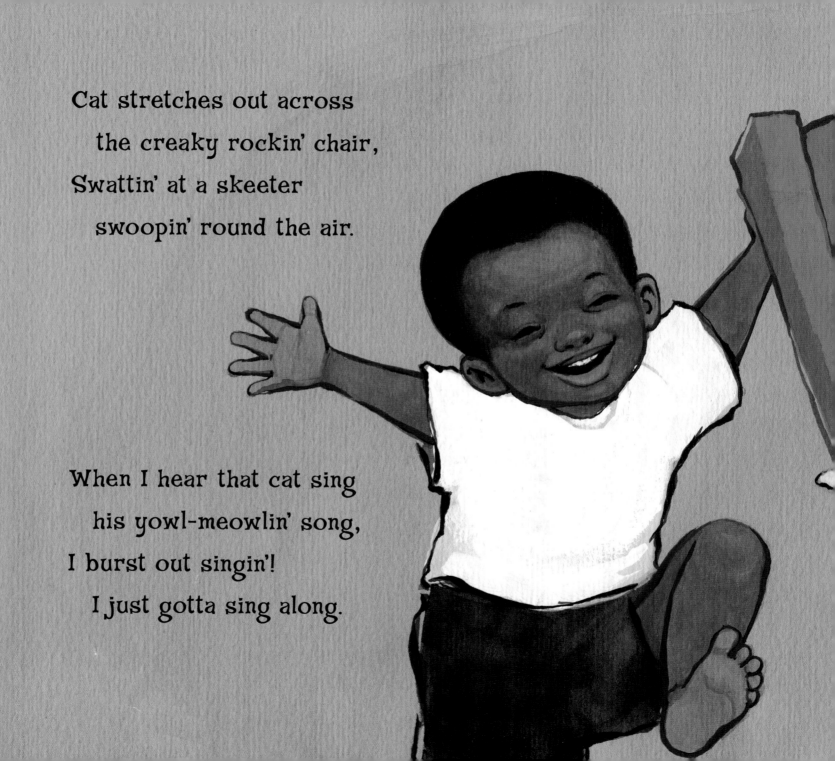

Yowl, growl, mew, meowl!

How I love to hoot and howl!

Daddy swings up the stairs, whistlin' all the way,
Scoops me up and asks me what I did all day.
When I hear my daddy sing his home-at-last song,
I burst out singin'! I just gotta sing along.

Tweetle-deet! Tootle-ooh!

I'm so glad to see you!

Mama's mixin' up a special suppertime treat.

Calls us to the table when it's ready to eat.

When I hear my mama sing
  her home-cookin' song,

I burst out singin'!
  I just gotta sing along.

Knife and fork,
spoon and dish!
What a feast—
it smells delish!

Baby snuggles into her cradle for the night,
Lookin' like a flower bud
   wrapped up warm and tight.
When I hear our baby sing
   her gurgle-coo song,
I burst out singin'!
I just gotta sing along.

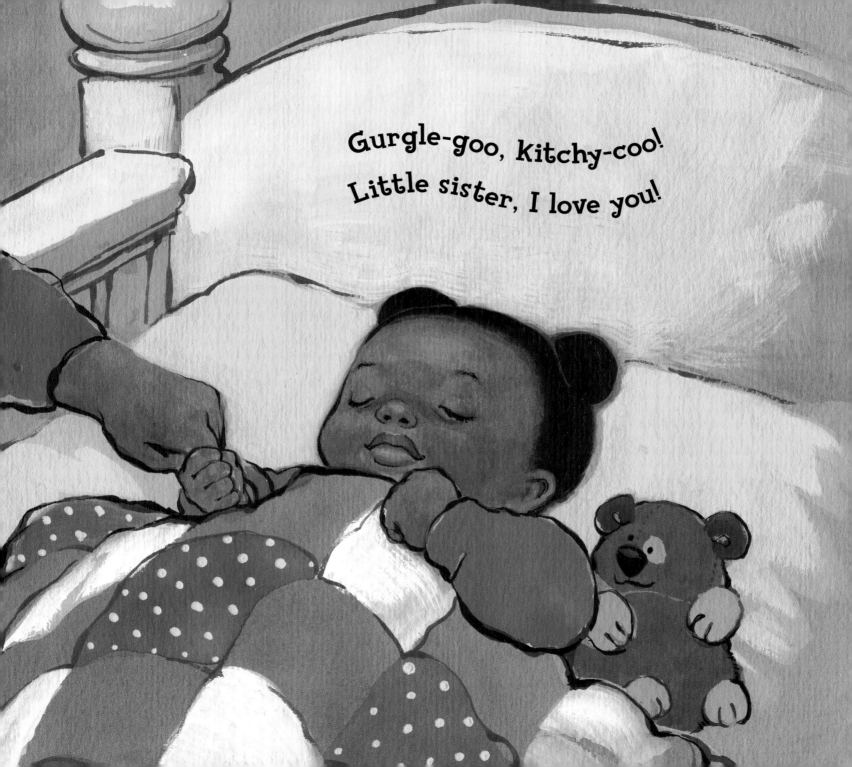

Gurgle-goo, kitchy-coo!
Little sister, I love you!

Stars begin to shimmer,
and the moon climbs the sky.
I hum a merry medley
from the day gone by.
Tomorrow, I'll sing another
sing-along song,
'Cause when I hear music,
I just gotta sing along.

Moon and stars, shining bright,
Whisper softly, good night!